THE JOURNEY TO KAILASH

Mike Allen

Copyright © 2008 by Mike Allen

All Rights Reserved.

Cover Artworks:
Illustration for *The Inferno*, Canto 29 by Gustave Doré, c. 1861

"Royal Elephant at the Gateway to the Jami Masjid, Mathura" by Edwin Lord Weeks, circa 1895

Cover Design Copyright © 2008 by Mike Allen

ISBN-13: 978-1-934648-45-2
ISBN-10: 1-934648-45-0

Trade Paperback

June 15, 2008

A Publication of
Norilana Books
P. O. Box 2188
Winnetka, CA 91396
www.norilana.com

Printed in the United States of America

The Journey to Kailash

Curiosities

an imprint of

Norilana Books

www.norilana.com

Also by Mike Allen

DEFACING THE MOON

PETTING THE TIME SHARK

DISTURBING MUSES

STRANGE WISDOMS OF THE DEAD

As editor:

NEW DOMINIONS:
Fantasy Stories by Virginia Writers

THE ALCHEMY OF STARS:
Rhysling Award Winners Showcase
(with Roger Dutcher)

MYTHIC

MYTHIC 2

CLOCKWORK PHOENIX
(forthcoming)

गणेथ

The Journey to Kailash

कैलाथ प्रवत

Mike Allen

for Richard Dillard

Contents

[misfortune when he leaves: his shadows grow to meet her]

The Journey to Kailash 3
Tithonus on the Shore of Ocean 9
Charon Finds a Woman on the Gridshore 13
Sisyphus Walks 18
Secret Infernos 21
Bacchanal 22
Giving Back to the Muse 24
deathmask 25
Time Triptych 26
Petals 28
Saturn Devours His Children 30
The Golden Helmet 32
Der Maulkorb 37
The Thirteenth Hell 38
Ghosts of the Apocalypse 39
The Disturbing Muses 40

[as the stars die, sad whispers stir the breeze]

Manifest Density 49
The Asteroid Painter 50
A Curtain of Stars 52
Pulse 53
Black Holes Hold Their Breath 54
Watching the Pot 55
Strange Cargo 56
retrovirus 58
Disaster at the BrainBank™ ATM 60
Munchausen vs. the Aliens 61

The End of the Affair 62
A Million Layers Removed 63
Requited 64
lis pendens 65
The Strip Search 66
Ectoppliances 68
Mrs. Rigsby's Fatecast 69
No One 70
Assembling Zembla 72
Planeta do Favela 73
The Captive Pleads with the Memory Carver 74
Midnight Rendezvous, Boston 76
Midnight Rendezvous, Philly 77
Midnight Rendezvous, Eden 79

[staring down the sun: the end he never sees]

Defacing the Moon 83
Freebasing the Moon 84
Sackful of Satellites 86
Retracing the Moon 87
Anointing the Time Shark 88
Petting the Time Shark 90
Eating the Time Shark 91
The Hollow Sphere 93
Escher's Bed 95
Miró's Mirror 96
Tanguy's Pebble 98
Klee's Garden 101
Chagall's Lamp 104
Picasso's Rapture 107
Pollock's Knives 113
O'Keeffe's Bones 118
Mondrian's War 120

misfortune when he leaves:
his shadows grow to meet her

The Journey to Kailash

When Ganesh marries my mother,
I am 18, my own man
in the eyes of the law; but barely a zygote
in his eyes. He calls me *spermling*
the first time we speak in private;
I tell him I know a doctor
who can do something about that nose.
Trunk curls up, perhaps to strike?
— a smile beneath
that touched the ancient folds around his eyes.
Kid, he says, *we'll get along fine.*

In my neighborhood, unseen trains
shake the ground every day at 5.
Streets without sidewalks slide between houses
tiny as boxcars, or old and rambling
as the stories the fogeys at the gas station tell,
like them eaten from inside and about to fall,
unlike them divided into 4 apartments each.
Ganesh and I play Xbox
before my afternoon shifts (of course he's great,
with all those hands he's at least two players
at once) and I steal glances
at his impossible profile, framed
by the dusty window: lumpy wrinkled nose
like a seasoned draft guard, curled
in inverse question mark of concentration;
on this day, clad in coveralls
with the bib undone: *How is it*, I wonder,
that you feel like you belong?

As if he heard, he mumbles,
Wherever someone loves me, I'm in like Flynn.

No, no, Mom, I don't want to know
(but as always, she tells me —
I know, he could use a few weeks at the Y,
and yeah, he's a lot older than your father
but turn off the lights
and you wouldn't know it. Sure,
sometimes the beginning is way better
than the end, but who cares
when he gets the party rolling . . .
Oh, when he gets rolling . . . and that trunk!)
No, no, Mom, I don't want to know . . .

I still don't have a clue how they met.
Mom can't remember, and my stepdad
always changes the subject, spins me
yet another harrowing first-person account
of leading his father's troops against demonkind.
For me there was no warning: after a long
afternoon behind the Burger King counter
I come home, to find him on the couch,
Mom asleep against his pillowy chest,
a bowl of popcorn in his lap, quietly munching;
his huge ears fanned out, cupped forward
as he watches *Temple of Doom* on cable
and giggles under his breath. In retrospect
I was far less surprised than
what the moment warranted.

As we wait in matching tuxes
for the justice of the peace to call us in
I feel new respect, even affection —
he didn't have to do this, we all know it,
but he agreed without a gripe when Mom asked.

See, kid, he whispers around a tusk,
your mother, she has this vivaciousness, *this* pluck,
this drive to defy all odds and plow on
that's like a bath of rakta chandan
for pranapratishhtha — *she makes me feel*
alive, you understand? This aatma
I want to catch with all my hands, and when
it flutters, let it go, watch its flight in awe,
then catch it again. An essence such as that
pumps new blood through an old heart.
Do you comprehend?
                              I nod "I do." *I knew*
you would, he says. *You have it too.* An arm
around my shoulders; three more hands
pinch my cheeks. *Too bad you're not a woman.*
A grin, a wink. The moment nearly ruined,
but some part of me still flattered.
After the vows and the happy tears, he lifts
his trunk to kiss me wetly on one ear.

My son, he says.
At the reception, for the first time, I see him dance.
No wonder Mom can't get enough.

* * *

You would think,
with a household god,
(of great luck and strong starts, yet!)
that I wouldn't still be slaving behind
the grease-smeared Burger King counter
(to be honest, I'm in dual-job hell;
come night, *yo no quiero Taco Bell*.)
I finally ask him about this lack of riches,
and he sighs and blinks those dewy eyes.
Spermling — he wags his trunk — *it don't work*

-5-

like that. Luck, okay, luck, is when
you're driving in downtown Manhattan, fighting
for every gap that opens in all that hurtling metal,
and your car, it's been threatening to stall
since the last tollbooth on the Jersey Turnpike,
and you made it, but your tank's on Empty,
and you beg that car, Please don't die —
and it's like it hears you, like its packed with prana,
and goes twenty miles further than possible,
and just when you feel rigor mortis
in the gas pedal, there is a pump station
at this *corner, that you didn't see seconds ago —*
and the $20 you thought you dropped
at the rest stop is in your pocket after all.
All four hands spread wide.
That's what luck is all about.

You would think, given all the above,
that I'd have never come home
in the early a.m. to find Mom
in the kitchen dark, crouched
over the cooking sherry, her silent tears
revealed when the lights come on.
What's wrong with me, she asks.
Is there some little demon inside me
that refuses to believe I deserve this?
Why don't I want to be happy?
I ask, *is it the other wives?*
She shakes her head.

* * *

How distracted he seems when he's present;
how lost she seems when he's gone.

Mothers, he grumps one morning
and pauses *Halo* to rest his chin on his hands.
No, not yours.
              Some mothers sure do hate
to give up their sons.
                    Did I ever tell you
what my mother did to me?
                          A dirty trick.
It was, you know, long before time
really got rolling, and I was playing with
my kitten, and I played with her a little
too rough (but I didn't mean to, see,
it had only been a few years since
Shiva first fused my head on).

I came home and my mom was bleeding
from her bindi, and when I asked what's wrong
she says to me, what ever I do to any ladki
I do to her. How cruel a thing
to do to a son! But I was still young,
didn't see it that way then. So I vowed
to never ever marry.
                    Well.
A few millenniums of celibacy
will make you decide there's some consequences
you can live with. So I took three wives —
take that, Mom! — but you'd think by now
she'd forgive me. Her unhappiness,
well, sometimes it still comes through.

He offered me the remains of his beer
(I refused) then polished it off with a chug,
and lamented:
Is it so hard for a mother to want
eternal happiness for her Dumbo-headed boy?

I haven't shared a word of this with Mom,
and won't.
I look at these checks I drag home,
compute how they add up with hers,
and know
we need every bit of luck we can hold onto.

But one late sleepless night
I Googled my stepfather and gawked
at hundreds of prettified statues and
read about Ganesh Chaturthi;
days of hymns and feasting,
red silk and red ointment,
the eleventh day my stepdad's image
submerged in the sea, symbolizing
his journey home to Kailash
bad luck drawn away like pilot fish
following his wake.
And I love him so
that I can't bring myself to ask him yet:
is it when he *leaves*
that misfortune truly goes away?

for John Peery

Tithonus on the Shore of Ocean

> *He feels himself to be*; a continent
> lapped everywhere by our amniotic flood
> — D.M. Thomas, *Tithonus*

SAN JOSE, SEPT. 26, 1984 — I or someone else
volunteered to slip back to the womb
my best friend [or stranger/pusher]
offered me a test swim in his sensory depr[a]vation tank
in there afloat I became
a continent independent
magma mass in rebellion
bubbling away from time's worm-crusted ocean floor

above that ragged abyss I swam at whatever speed I chose
the plane ride home [7-hour flight]
took no more than 2, it seemed
but I could not maintain that blessed buoyancy,
sank back
into the jagged bed of realtime
and never could rise again
   .
   .
   .
   Perhaps then why I
   [or someone else]
   chose this choice
   classic brainjam
   mind in a jar,
   nerves severed,
   body shed.

[i] without input, rhythm, context
risen so far I perceive no surface
to clue me as to whether I move
1st person limited point of view
wandering the convolutions inside
what's [maybe] my own mind
no measurable timeflow to defy

.

.

.

      Seconds or centuries later,
I came aware, [be]came aware
of a universe, one or several
      stacked in baklava layers
      brimming with entities

at first only perceivable as moving points
      abstract plankton
then brighter, strange running lights
glowfish hunting in an abyss darker than deathnight
brighter still, more numerous, even more
void in Van Gogh chaos
whorls   streaks   starbursts
intense as blinding reflections
infinite as ignorance
speedy as cicada killers
milling like Calcutta traffic

[i] without eyes
marveled at these swarmschools
certain they were other minds [human?]
unveiled in my New Ocean
my efforts to float in
      their direction   all directions
stubbornly remained equidistant
I stretched/strained for

for anyone   for any one   for all
again again again repeat again
.

.

.

Seconds or centuries unfolded
bloomed
in a bursting bulge of will & wish
all grew closer at once
drawn in [or me drawn out]
by the voodoo of my desire

Can a continent
overflow its banks
and flood the ocean?

torrent of I
tsunam[i]self
wave
taller
deeper
broader
than all the island motes of self-awareness
that form the nuerons in god's schizophrenic brain
.

.

.

In millennia or milleseconds
I became the message and the medium
invading and connecting
3.5 trillion minds at once
the list of *what* washed through me
emotions
sensations
revelations
degradations

        agonies & glories
        ecstasies
        & boredoms
would tick on for eons

all the glowfish shine the same color now
movements much more regimented
tragic or maybe just inevitable

        Poor Argus, unthinking brute
        with so many eyes open at once
        how could he narrow down
                the direction
from which god's murderous messenger approached?

[it's impossible to be/see]
[so many]
[and stay focused on the linear]

so I've chosen this history
to give myself dimension and direction
after some arbitrary interval
I may choose another
                .
                .

                .

                being god is all about
                finding ways to pass time
                & stay sane

Charon Finds a Woman on the Gridshore

With all our minds sped to a state
where mere fragments of a second stretched to eternities
in a kingdom of invented incident,
simulations of every existence imaginable,
none of the multimultitudes quivering in data rapture
noticed how the flood of minds from the Outside had
        thinned to a stream, a trickle,
then single droplets in a dry abyss.

But I knew. For the Harvesters made me Ferryman.

I, made Charon, piloted my boat across the shimmering —
skimming the surface of the Rapture,
inviting the newly downloaded onto creaking timbers,
my vessel capable of holding thousand who were never aware
of their superimposition, always thinking themselves
        the sole soul aboard.

I would not take them to another shore.
we would float till they understood the wonder or futility
and then submerge, their matrixes swept beneath
to join the binary river.
And always their disembodied bodies shared tales
of the reverence reserved for the Harvest Nodes;
cults of millions swarming the Western mountains,
killing themselves to prove their purity
to genetically-engineered acolytes with cleft cat faces,
clicking camera eyes, those who manned the offering
of bodies to the sacrificial tables.

* * *

But finally, no passengers came, no bathers for the Styx.

* * *

I have dreamed in the datastream for billions of lifetimes
and I recall them all; unlike the other downloads,
    I never choose erasure.
Thus the electrons in my matrix simulate surprise,
still possible, even now, when in the midst of my latest life
    iteration —
this time, a simple farmer, rousing my children to tend
to the stinking barn in the hour before cockcrow —
my boat appears around me, spontaneous shell,
and I glide across prismatic data gold, bound for Gridshore.
Dataflux generates scent; the Rapture
reminds me of oranges, of woodsmoke, of copper.
Do these same scents stimulate the lone gray figure
huddling on the Gridshore's black banks (they can
be any texture at all, but this time they are sand.)

The machines birthed her in the same garb
that they consumed her in; shapeless woolen dress
cinched at the waist with colorless cord;
sickly grey gauze stretched over her mouth and eyes,
draped over her hair; her gender betrayed
where the slashed fabric droops, her mortality
betrayed by black bloodstains.

She fears me; she runs; though she soon finds
any direction she picks bring her closer.
The neverspace will join us in inevitable meeting.
Yet the way she shrinks, even as the prow of the ferry
slides onto the sand by her feet;
she did not come willingly.
How did she come at all?

I gesture to the flowing gold of Rapture, speak welcome
        inside her.
She screams, a burst of single-digit code
darting through me, harmless tachyon beam,
lost in less than an instant in the data stream.

I let go of my oar, reach out in greeting,
reach into her, weaving my matrix through hers
to bring understanding from within. I learn:

that her grey is uniform, a uniform imposed inside and out
a greyness of mind, enveloping fog, smog of unlearning
roils thickly through the minds of humanity's fearful
        remnants
in the world the Harvest Nodes freed us both from.

She does not know where she is.
Contemplating the wonders of age-old but still miraculous
        technology,
comprehending even a simple machine, or even
an attempt to grasp written words,
as alien, as forbidden, as unthinkable
as uncovering her face.

These machines that form universe to billions are forgotten
        — almost . . .
Words form, descriptors of terror:
Those That Hunger Below the Earth
Spirit Swallowers, Black Iron Pits,
Prisons of the Lost, where souls are melted
and recombined, poured into molds that spit
out legions of long-fanged, slit-eyed mutants,
the packs that hunt in craggy valleys
and across overgrown plains, scouring for
humanity's dwindled remains.
(I learn why the Harvest Nodes are so reviled:

so many came to live inside that we gave
the world to the descendants of the Guardians;
not enough humans left to keep them controlled.)

Her people, hardscrabble hunters and gatherers
starving off the lean of the land, erected their village
in forgotten caverns upslope in the hills of Kalifor;
but not forgotten or secret enough.
The nomads came, with their fangs and wiry helmets,
their lances full of deadly light,
their steeds like leather-hided octopi,
probing in the dark through every nook and hiding place
to draw out shrieking captives;
her fear drove her back to tunnel forbidden by her elders
(now dead); but not before
she saw her aging mother raped for sport,
her infant son shredded like a hated cloth doll;
she backed into the smooth tunnel that the elders
claimed lead straight to damnation;
slid into a chamber of strange lights,
failed to understand creaks of long-dormant machinery;
shrieked as the probes bore down through her veil.

I try to teach her all I know, but the waters
of my knowledge part about her rock, flow past.
She cannot grasp the meanings of technology
She has no framework to comprehend
the purpose of the harvest nodes,
the relief the downloads gave to billions.
But she can understand Forever.
She can understand that the consequences
her elders warned of had come to pass.
Her matrix a shriek of impulse or terror,
she climbs the side of my sturdy boat,
lets herself fall into the Rapture,
because she understands

there is no other choice ahead.
At once she is gone.

* * *

And at once the datastream returns me to dreaming.

* * *

Not once in our exchange
did I learn the contours of her face
and perhaps, through all these infinities,
I never will.

for Charlie Saplak

Sisyphus Walks

Sisyphus lifts the thighbone of a god
above his head (a bone thick and long as
a felled tree) and begins his trudge
across the hard-packed dust.

Spills of silver fluid blanket uneven stone,
not pooling in hollows but spreading in
thin film atop the ground, slick sheets
draped over surface, that part rather than
splash as Sisyphus steps through.

Pipes, metal, ceramic, cracked, of
unpredictable diameter rise from valley floor
as breathing tubes from water; some protrude
through mounds of bone. Ragged
openings echo voices from some
place deep below, their syllables
forming no language Sisyphus knows.

Sheer black rock bluffs rise from the plain,
jagged walls carving empty ocean basin
into this bewildering maze where Sisyphus
is never lost as he walks, titan bone
balanced over head, around and over other
Cyclopean remains, charred pelvises or ribs,
a jaw bone that rocks itself, still eager to speak,
fingers long as Sisyphus' legs crooking
Come Hither. Sisyphus has seen all before
and ignores.

From these bleak walls towers rise, not built
so much as grown, or eroded, stalagmites
stabbing into oilslick sky. At intervals,
massed clusters rise as castles, their rough
battlements riddled with windows, round portholes
peppered at random, even bored into unsculpted
bluffs; sometimes faces peer from them,
bestial visages, or smooth masks, or things
much more indistinct. They never speak, and in
a blink have gone. On them, Sisyphus
wastes no wonder.

Shadows in the maze constantly change,
thrown by whatever arc the spines of the sun
choose to sweep as it twists and squirms
cross-sky, a glowing wyrm whose radiance
brings no heat, its soft progress sometimes
thwarted by coils of sickly rainbow cloud,
sometimes whipped along in eddies
of a firmament where colors never blend.
Like Sisyphus the sun never settles or sets,
merely strains against confinement, thrashing
to all compass points and back again.
Sisyphus remembers a moon, complex
mobile of cold beauty, intricate pieces that
spun and interwove; but like the night,
it's banished; he can't remember when
he last saw it shimmer above.

Pushing against the grain of a wind
that sucks and blows as breath,
Sisyphus arrives at last at neat fields
carved at random by castle shadows.
This is his destination, though no place of rest.
Among the ordered rows of bone
he walks, until he comes to a tract where

parts of a behemoth skeleton
lie ceremonially on the ground,
arranged as one should be;
shoulders above ribs, feet below knees;
gingerly, he lowers thighbone into place.
No arms yet, no hands, no head.

Sisyphus walks away, with countless
more bones to search among
to find and collect the right ones.

Once this god is together again,
perhaps it will tell him why it placed
him here, why night never comes,
whether Sisyphus has at last
repaid his long-forgotten debt.
And if it has no such to say,
then he will begin again
with another one.

Secret Infernos

in the walls of the haunted asylum
    the inmates mingle and socialize

    freed from the blinding fog of body
voices unlimbered from the bindings of throat

unafraid to let their shattered psyches' shapeless limbs
    overlap, blend, share
words the way teenage girls share makeup

souls once shredded and alone
    woven together in a tattered tangle
    spreading through the space behind cinderblock

like undetected fires

secret infernos
    of discovery and celebration

Bacchanal

he traded his robe for a lab coat
its filthy tail
sweeps through oil-sheened mud
flaps with back alley lurch
spine hunched in huddled conspiracy
hooves split bleeding
a black bile wine
reeled everywhere on the tainted ley lines
blind husk heeds
the zombie century call
hopes the fix fixes all
hops the walls
prints trickle behind
rolled up sleeves reveal
the needle
tracks of self consumption
sore of entry throbs
purple jellyfish
hissing mob slithers behind
hollow-eyed   supermodel squad
anexoria hot   pop singer dirty
wilted parrot plumage
used-up Maenads
hunting for another Orpheus
no talent required   any orifice will do
pop'n'play in the master bedroom
to the music artery beat   mad-eyed
waif kneels curls fragile fingers
in the wool of His hips
boy   girl   no matter

liberate the libation
gunshots outside   the undead
can't wait their turn
cultists sweating and trembling
in the Superdome
the worst of this generation
the best of this generation
bored to distraction
conjure Him   in the seedy glade
of tire ruts   beer cans   broken glass   hymens
clumsily torn
see the horns on his haggard head
glint in the headlights
of the pickup truck
sticks into snakes for everyone
curl them round your arm
to raise a vein
discover something new to do
for true   we're all born again
grown on our fathers' thighs
like a cancer

Giving Back to the Muse

She wears a necklace of knives and eyes,
a sash sewn from flags and faces,
boots welded from bomb fragments,
a belt of hangman's rope.
You fear she'll see you watching
but you can't look away,
not even once she notices your stare.
She *is* medium cool; she requires
all your senses to impart the vision,
stab your eyes, shred your feet,
strangle you in half and burn your face away.
Your sinuses crack like eggshells.
Your loins avalanche blood.
You put your tongue in her mouth,
let her chew and swallow. What use
were your words ever anyway?

deathmask

This morning, I choose blindness.
The face I pull on has no holes for eyes.
Many times before I've worn
this mask of flesh; it's ragged now,
calloused and raw against my fingertips.
I stroke the stitches at my temples.
threads that give this skin its shape.

The mirror I can't see chides me:

You've left too much bone exposed.
At least fix your forehead where
it sags loose.
              Then the mirror groans:
Why this face again, all purple-bruised?
Why not the Green Woman
with leaves for cheeks and blooms for eyes?
Why not the cold white oval
that makes you such an elegant ghost?
Why not the Laughing Owl
or Coy-Eyed Cat? Why always
must you pick the most difficult way?
You'll stumble through the castle halls,
one hand always in the dust beneath
the portraits, sure to frighten off
any escort who might offer aid.

But this one's soft as silk, I say.
It feels best. It hurts least.

Time Triptych

Three hours after midnight:
the witching hours, when
the world's veil grows thin;
ghosts shed their masks
and clocks speak their powers.
Three hours this night share their stories:

I.

The clock on the nightstand
shifts its red fingers,
signing that the end of this encounter
moves a minute closer.
Your hand on my arm, asking me
to force the minutes back.
And so I do.
They strain in my grip,
forced to bend the wrong way,
knuckles folded backward by a bully.
How that makes you smile.

II.

The pendulum of night's clock
swings down while darkness still presides,
leaving nothing but the hungry stars
to leer above the trees.
Among the roots, things crawl,

drawn by the call of emptiness before sunrise.
Their rustling stirs the woman buried
in the glass box, her endless sleep shaken
with dreams of prickly kisses
and crumbs of herself borne off
to sate wicked queens.

III.

The old woman frightened me.
She only meant to make me laugh,
but in the way she moved her face
to mock the tall clock's toll,
eyes bulged out, mouth an eerie O,
I felt the deathwatch beetle
whisper in her skin,
the ticking I imagined
from Poe's tale of vulture eyes
and vengeful hearts, the rhythm
my own pulse sounds in the dark.

Petals

field of memories
flickers, blooms brushed
by charnel winds;
desperate to preserve
what searing gusts
leave behind,
I crawl amid
the vein-dark stalks
that sting my
hands, my face;
I crawl amid
the nettled stalks
to find the flowers,
to eat:

petals from
my island childhood,
papaya thick,
at first breadfruit sweet
but bright yellow inside,
tinted with red ant fire,
full of wriggling legs
that struggle
in my throat;

petals from
my mountain boyhood,
tobacco tang,
coal bitter,
thorns hidden

in the creases,
blue as chill air,
blue as bruises
under skin of dust and mud;

petals from
the brink of manhood,
white as paper
and as dry;
the salt of lust,
phloem of love;
visions burst on the tongue,
blood-red hope,
blood-red despair,
flavor the same;

petals from
my middle age,
blackened before
I arrive:
brittle ash,
peeled paint,
crust that crumbles
as I pluck;
who could want
such tasteless dregs?

I blow a kiss,
scatter the petals,
share them with the wind
that sears my face.

Saturn Devours His Children

El sueño de la razón produce monstruos.
— Francisco Goya

I watch the black goat-man dance around the fire
before spirits twisted with fear-filled desire.
I can't hear their manic laughter, but I see —
through the walls of this house I see their screams.

Leocadia, my dearest, who would now believe
you are the same beauty for whom I once risked death,
my ageless Maja of supple thighs and soft pale breasts
for whose image the Inquisitor wished me charred

two long decades ago? Perhaps he knew the sin in you
ran deeper than bare hips and mischievous eyes.
Infernal one, Leocadia was never your name,
but your true name I will not learn, so it will do.

Observe these two old men that I have placed
beside the window, how one leans close, his lips
brush so intimately beneath the other's ear.
These phantoms, etched in dust on void,

are you and I, Leocadia . . . but it's you who tilts
your head as if to listen, and I who drains soul's nectar
from your neck. What small sacrifice I have made
for your sweetly cursed sorcery, this sight that left me deaf

but lights the universe's secret shadows bright
as solstice moons, shows me the giant whose footsteps

toppled cities of Spain, the djinn who battle in the clouds
for our souls, the monsters that flap from our heads

when we sleep. I marvel, my Leocadia, at your contentment.
Playing my mad muse feeds you more, it seems,
than the hordes of souls who have served as your wine
in the banquet of dreams. If you chose me, one night,

Leocadia, as your partner, offered me death in your arms,
let me shudder out my life against your unearthly flesh,
I would gladly come. But you will not make prey, you
say, of one you truly love. My death, you leave to another.

As I bring your fingertips to my lips, dearest one, I wonder
what alien thoughts must swim behind those timeless eyes,
as you watch old man Saturno gnaw your love away,
as Time most surely devours all his mortal children.

The Golden Helmet

1. The Streetwalker

Addled in midmorning by
the fermented demons that always keep him company,
Henri staggers in his shuffling way
into *le pays des fées*
or so he thinks for a sun-blinded moment.

But, no, he's merely traipsed into
his neighbor's opulent garden, confronting
damask roses and prized white tulips
and this sinuous creature draped across
Monsieur Forest's fat lap.
A casual visitor, street wanderer
seeking new business, she is
mere flesh,
though flesh grown strange; intriguing flower
astounding his jaded eye.

Her blond locks twine up into a teardrop
that gleams with solid sheen, a golden helmet
not far removed from the priceless cap of Helios.
But no sun creature is she; it's an imp's hat
that grows from her head.
*Had Bosch painted fairies, he might
have dreamed you up*, thinks Henri.
An ill-used refugee from the mound, yes,
yet fey nonetheless. Wear and tear
of the kind only Montemartre brothels can induce
seam her face, her neck, but her wicked smile

smooths all into a mask of antique, even ancient mischief.
On sight of Henri she springs,
astonishes him a second time, as she takes his hand,
the one that holds the brush,
stoops to meet his eyes,
kneels to regard his palm.

A flitting fingertip traces the lines:
the contact of her skin on his
like strokes of alizarin crimson through cool green.
You are the last of your kind, she says.
A thousand years of power and darkness run in your blood.
Bad things wished to break you spirit,
but only your body could they touch, and now
you become the unrepentant fool,
the jester beloved by all the kingdom, the bonfire
that lights this mad pageant of flesh.

Dans quel vin noierons-nous ce vieil ennemi?
Dis-le, belle sorcière! says Henri,
slurring his Baudelaire.
Fey one, you have captured me. Now let me
in turn trap you forever.
                              And he painted her
in her Chinese peasant's blouse and golden helmet
as easily as a mere mortal drums his fingers
or scratches an itch.

Late that afternoon,
he is for a third time amazed
when she kneels, silent, between his malformed legs
to ply her trade,
to steal a part of him away.

2. The Circus

Such a mood etched upon him;
when he waddles into
the cafés, the dance halls,
the peepshows, the whorehouses,
when the patrons spy his stunted form
— bespectacled bearded gnome,
stumps of legs supporting a grown man's torso
— and begin to laugh,
he laughs with them,
their laughter an offering he accepts,
a tribute of recognition.

He has become Montmartre's carnal spirit,
joyfully deformed,
generously corrupt,
gleefully debauched,
celebrating the body in all its pouched, plump, pocked
        imperfections,
its ringmaster and its historian,
recording the human whirlwind:
gaudy hats and billowing blouses,
the green haze of absinthe,
sagging rumps and shocks of red pubic hair,
monsieurs emerging from beneath sheets
to kiss their rented lovers,
the stark black of slumming aristocrats,
slipping away from the life he left behind for good
to test with cowardly fingers
the seething waters that were now his home.

Jester and lord in one, he sketched at the tables,
his head often cradled in the bosom
of a slender lady-in-waiting draped in fine white,
merely his due

through the short years of his reign.
Montemartre opened to him its deepest intimacies.
None turned him away.

3. The Clown

In a year, he will draw a pistol
and put bullets through the tiger-sized spiders
that will crawl out of his delirium
onto his bedroom walls.
And five after that, the success of his last
long-term undertaking: self-inflicted
death by drink.
But for now he is the darling of the press.
His wicked posters are the talk of the truly chic.

Holding court one hazy evening
among his subjects in the Rue des Moulins
he sees a glint of gold beyond the top hats,
blond hair twined into a teardrop.

His imp crowned with the sun's golden helm
fastening her bright yellow bodice,
her supple shoulderblades exposed, and more,
a tantalizing hint
closed off and concealed.
She is somehow younger, smoother,
wrapped in baggy black,
torso draped in puffy yellow cascade
that part for a ravine of cleavage.
She is no longer a peasant but a clown, and yet
Henri can't mistake that strange flower
that so enthralled him.

She finds a bench, slumps,
legs spread wide, regards the throng with glazed eyes.
She won't remain alone long.

He wonders as he trundles her way
whether the light in her has died,
whether the poxes and opiates that collect dues at the
        circus door
have taken this one's toll, but no,
her gaze finds him, and there:
that infernal grin of recognition
he returns, but falters, her bared teeth
transmuted
her teeth bared, like the dead
whose lips have withered away
as she points his way
and laughs
and laughs
great mocking howls
black tears streaming down
her greased white face
beneath eyes that never blink,
and he feels again
the agony of thighbones breaking,
feels his realm flip beneath him,
Rumpelstiltskin freak whose true name lies exposed,
still the Fool, but King no more.

As she completes her theft
he swoons, stumbles to kneel
between her obscene feet, and even
though she has vanished, her laughter spreads,
surrounding him now,
gathered in new voices.
Her eyes still burn,
alizarin fire
in the deep green of his drowning.

Der Maulkorb

They paraded the scold through
dusty streets with a metal cage
clamped to her head, bridle collar
locked tight around her neck,
hooks anchored in her tongue,
pretty bells hung from her mask
to ring her passage to the peasantry;
still foolish enough to protest,
her noises fit for fine comedy —
the onlookers' laughter tells you that
as they queue up for the spectacle.

Centuries and an ocean away
I brush dust off the counter top,
watch sunlight highlight the motes
as they churn through our silence; you
long since learned not to test
this cage I've welded or the barbs
that transfix your voice. Partners
in farce, we face each other, wielding
forks to stab morsels served as stand-ins
& lick the blooded tines. Anyone watching
would surely laugh themselves sick.

The Thirteenth Hell

Her voice in my ear said, *look, look*.
Though I squeezed my eyelids shut,
hid my face in my hands, I could still see it.

I pressed my fingernails in,
hooked my thumbs and pulled,
like so many here before. And
she said *look*, and I could still see it.

I crawled to the wall,
slammed my head on the stone,
found the cracks in the bone and clawed.
Her voice in my brain said, *look*,
and I could still see it.

I scrabbled at the ground
turned soft by my blood,
made a hole deep enough to force
my head in. She whispered from the earth,
look, look, and I could still see it.

The mud has swallowed me.
Things there feast on what's left
of what I used to be. And she
is one of them, her mouth moving
in my skull. *Look*, she breathes, *look*,
and I can still see it.

for Laird Barron

Ghosts of the Apocalypse

Hell is a haunted world
where only ghosts remain
to stir the dust.

Hell is a haunted sun
swollen red to swallow
shame-filled eons.

Hell is a haunted star:
spirit remnants gravity-chained
as it spins apart.

Hell is uncounted ghostly voices
silenced in emptiness.

The Disturbing Muses

Nodding by night around my bed,
Mouthless, eyeless, with stitched bald head.
— Sylvia Plath

A. *canto d'amore*

Where did he find them, stone-gowned goddesses
who half a life later would bear
silent witness as their despairing disciple
swallowed poisoned air?

In the City of the Faceless he left them,
burned the maps that charted his return,
even burned those engraved on his skin.
He peeled their lacquer from his hand
that held the brush, nailed the bleeding glove
to a wall, beneath some blind and nameless
emperor's reproachful stare.

What she could not stop herself
from embracing,
he fled.
Behind him they tracked without eyes.
One howled
from the mouth that opened between its breasts
a word
shaped in the echo chamber of its heart
with no beginning or end.

B. *malinconia della partenza*

Amnesia through repetition:
that dour drooping face presided sadly
over copy after copy;
three dummy-headed dolls, their sorcery
badly diluted through decades
of insincere self-forgery.
His detractors said he whored his past for money.
He gladly let them believe it so.
Perhaps even he believed this so;
self-mocking at the end, passing off
bleak green skies as funny,
teasing artifice, a wry prank of the soul.

But six decades before
staring up at that sick twilight
he didn't find it funny at all.
Could he recall when it became
late afternoon forever,
when the long shadows froze?
Yes: the sick pain in his belly
still unsubsided, staring at the sculpture
of Dante in the Piazza Santa Croce
when the day itself coalesced
into marble and darkness.

Hours or days, he wandered:
the light never changed.
Moving enigmas, sails or trains
drifted soundless behind walls,
their cargoes hidden; he could not find
the other side, no more than he
could find a living soul.
                    Stumbling
among stark arcades, pale colonnades,

barren plazas, his survival
rested solely on an unseen denizen
who left food in incongruous places:
cluster of bananas beneath the aqueduct;
artichoke heads like war trophies
under the cannon barrel; pastries
found in places that defied the eye.

He thought, at one point, he had come
upon his savior: placed a hand on
the man's shoulder, turned him and
confronted blank mannequin face
with a single eye sketched
where brow should be.

Returned to bed, screaming,
believing he had seen the future.
The muses had made themselves known,
though he did not know it yet.
Still points of power,
triple nexus from which all stillness grew,
they awaited his arrival.

C. *archeologo*

Smokestacks stood watch on the horizon,
never breathing,
never close enough to touch.
Perspective was illusory
in this metaphysical space.
The profile of a face
seen outside the window
resolved itself as silhouette
of distant, impossible castle.

Still the food appeared.
Perhaps Ariadne herself —
her bare-breasted, resigned effigy
had so haunted him in Greece —
trying to lead him out of this time-twisted maze?
But every new exploration
brought him nearer to the heart, not away,
before the great red hand of the hour
swept him back.

Space made non sequitur:
Streets become walls,
tables become floors,
towers loom larger at distance
than up close. Here, entire ghettos
populated by crude mannequins;
there, mannequins as mountains,
bodies cobbled
from columned ruins.

Yet another empty piazza
beneath sinister green sky —
but what made these three blind muses
so magnify his unease?
Ruthless and primal,
stripped of all visage by the modern age.
One stood forever in shadow.
Did another shadow, smaller, dart behind?

No mouths with which to speak
but the silence itself chiseled words.

Bring us to her, it said.
Bring her to us.

A vision inside another's brain,
connected across the infinite,
transformed his own head.

D. *il sogno trasformato*

She found his painting somewhere humble,
a print in a book, stark black and white; and the same night
cowered beneath covers as three massive stone matriarchs
nodded above her knowingly. She dreamed
how their marble gowns enfolded her,
three mothers' overpowering embrace.

He knew

She dreamed her own face stitched shut,
skin tanned to leather thickness, implacable ovals
for mouth and eyes, rimmed with spiraling thread;
her slender form stiff as a tailor's dummy,
her blond tresses a wig anyone could remove and wear.

What hue

She dreamed herself again risen from ashes,
another failed attempt to do what she did best;
her red-haired vengeance, like Sisyphus' stone,
always rolling back on her. Flesh, bone,
but still nothing there.

He had painted

They kept eyeless vigil around her as she prepared;
their beautiful silence grew layered, an aching harmony
that approached the perfect stillness of immutable night.
They nodded approval as she stepped into their shadows,
turned the knob and opened the altar's door.

Her life, and despaired.

Now was the future, the future from which he fled,
    the future he fled into.

E. enigma dell'Oracolo

He painted, and copied, and copied,
and forgot the girl of his dreams.
Married a Russian immigrant after the wars,
her slender form still as a mannequin
as she posed for his brush,
her blond tresses ghostly on the canvas.

coda: mistero di una strada

At strange street's foot
a little girl in silhouette
runs with a hoop toward
a waiting shadow
which extends a stunted limb;
blacker and heavier than she,
it grows, as she ascends,
to meet her.

**as the stars die,
sad whispers warm
the breeze**

Manifest Density

Let's play a game of chicken with the Universe.
Let's extend our suburbs to the quasar edge.
Let's burrow condos into every moon,
open discount stores at each new sun,
carve two-way traffic tunnels throughout spacetime,
plan cul-de-sacs of gated nebulae.
Let's evangelize all unearthly aborigines.
(They too need Slurpee cups and no U-turns.)
Let's fill the empty saddle with ourselves.
And if we can't kickstart the Big Crunch with our Masses,
let's break bacchanal through all the thinning Cosmos
to keep each other warm as the stars die.

The Asteroid Painter

Knowing that decades in the future an asteroid will collide with our world, we seek to change that with Yarkovsky's effect, by choosing the most effective face to paint, using the sun's heat and our ingenuity to propel the rock toward some other destiny. *That* is our body's sole purpose.
— *Chair of the Painters, 2080 A.D.*

He knew himself to be
the greatest Yarkovskian painter
though none of his league
conceded it so.

    When the painting of asteroids
    to deflect orbits away from Earth
    evolved to something more
    than a survival exercise,

he outpaced all the rest,
as expert at the mental command
of the remote spraybrush across
gulfs of space as at coaxing

    contours to aid in shadow
    and highlight. Image after image
    he etched in paint trajectories
    upon barren, airless rock:

tigers, zebras, sumptuous nudes,
faces of dictators and presidents,

fierce yet sad self-portraits,
all sent tumbling beyond the sun's reach.

He defied his fellows who saw
these canvasses and their cold, distant
destinies as final freedom from
tyranny of form; making instead

a record for strangers' eyes,
strangers perhaps only imagined,
who might through their fantastic
telescopes spy what pigment remains,

and recognize the mark of the alien,
and wonder how, and wonder who.

In memory of George Solonevich

A Curtain of Stars

The needle repeats
with imperfect persistence
dotted thread lines,
new meridians in cloth,

stitches connections
between constellations,
binds warm lining
to a curtain of stars;

a seam that would
only compliment
the cloud-free night
should it appear there

suddenly crisscrossing
the Milky Way.
The spirits of the stars
are with us tonight

watching from the heart
of the fire; sparks rise
to the flue as you stitch
a new cosmos together.

Pulse

red pulse black pulse blue pulse sound thrums
quantum chance rhythm beats with subatomic
possibilities that pulse up pulse down pulse with

uncountable thousands of divisions in the stream
of time pounding a music of fate beating executing
the most unlikely steps on the gallows of wave

function probability procreation and intertwining
destiny testifying for a hopeless cause resisting
the pulse is like rejecting gravity like swimming

against the undertow of infinity it's best yes
to surrender to move to the rhythm of blood
of heartbeat of breath of desire of impetus to survive

that will which existed before consciousness still
stares out from the space between atoms made
of tones composed in probability scale notes

once compressed in the mote that made the big
band bang the sound that awakened all of everything
strung the cords of existence on the bars of time

and forced the music into pulsing motion

Black Holes Hold Their Breath

"I'm sorry to disappoint science fiction fans, but if information is preserved, there is no possibility of using black holes to travel to other universes. If you jump into a black hole, your mass energy will be returned to our universe, but in a mangled form, which contains the information about what you were like, but in an unrecognizable state."
— *Stephen Hawking, 2004*

Black holes hold their breath,
deny the urge to exhale
as life's pull grows frail;

speak at last in death
tall tales of their creation,
slow lives told in sighs;

slow gods' dying lies,
spewing misinformation,
hiding holocaust:

All the lives they've claimed
returned, recombined and maimed;
all escape hopes lost.

Damning stars, we curse
your crime: robbed of our chance to
slip the end of time.

Watching the Pot

Nagging suspicion makes you check
your scopes and dishes, but all's static,
just static heard through heaven's window.
Every day, you put your ear to the glass,
leave your eager oil-marks on its underside;
still no breath mists the window
from the other side. Yet you can't help
imagining that compound or cat-like
alien eye, leaning down on its stalk
to look around every time you turn away.

Strange Cargo

The train slides toward the hill-concealed horizon,
a mammoth serpent winding through the tall grass,
its strange steel-skeletal cars stacked with stranger cargo,
men and women, naked as newborns, crisscrossed eight high
in neat columns, interlocking puzzle towers of flesh.

Car thrown into park, I step out, squint down, but I'm
too far yet to tell whether I'm staring at slick synthetics
or true skin; they're perfect: trim and muscular, no
birthmarks to see, no moles, a eugenicist's wet dream;
yet sexless, static, faces blank as brain death,

a promenade of empty shells, automatons,
an android shipment, enough to fill a city, etch
personalities, watch a culture come to life. I wonder
what doctrines, what dogma, what commands
are waiting to be written on their minds?

A rich demagogue's androgynous harem, perhaps,
swarming their master like bees on their queen?
Or an instant cult, ready-made worshipers,
undying faithful to light torches in the catacombs?
Impervious soldiers, trained with a download,

storming distant deserts or jungle against others
of their own kind, or even others of mine?
Underwater miners or void-bound farmers
unafflicted by a need to breathe, raising air-filled
domes to make more space for their makers?

Pitiful, beautiful slaves, bound
for existence (hardly a life)
without choice; no one should wish
to be one of you, no — but why then
do I feel such envy?

retrovirus

no vault could hold it
no scientist keep it secret
too many people too eager
to set it loose
contagious as a slogan or a jingle
or an urban slang contraction
(which were first to go)

we lost our ethnic accents in the plague
voiceboxes locked in standard broadcast
with the occasional Bogart swagger
John Wayne drawl or Mayberry twang

& we lost our vulgar vocabularies
gasped again at Rhett Butler's nerve
& Lauren Bacall's lips

the virus ate our internet-inspired libidos
courtships reduced to smoldering stares
in town squares
& smart-aleck dialogue
climaxed in a kiss

& we lost our color vision
Only black & white & stark shadow
everyone knew again which hat they wore
& where they sat

& we buried in shrouds all unpatriotic doubts
& flew glory bound on wings of eagles:
Our way or the highway
I did it my way
Father knows best

Disaster at the BrainBank™ ATM

We're sorry, we've misfiled your personality,
and deposited your childhood memories
in someone else's account. We *warned* you:
we've just upgraded, you must protect
your own persona till the bugs smooth out.
It seems you've far surpassed your limit
In altruistic reverie, we've deducted two
life-changing epiphanies for each infraction
(our standard fee) and provided you with
four new subconscious anxieties as insurance
against our own liability. Now here's your requested
pleasure center stimulation. Have a Nice Daydream™.

Munchausen vs. the Aliens

Urban legends encounter urbane liar,
tractor-beam him
right off his five-winged pegasus;
five oval grey heads
roll at saber-flicks,
before they clamp the Baron down,
pierce him in place,
spread him open.
His cavities issue
oily polygonal beasts
too wily to be
imprisoned in specimen jars.

His vivisection completed,
he thanks greys with grace,
folds them with their saucer
into imaginary space,
sealed forever inside
a tale he spins
beside the hearth-light.

The End of the Affair

He tried to dispatch her
by leaving the wormhole
to the planet of razordemons
open behind her bathroom door.

She tried to dispatch him
with nanobots engineered
to turn the beer in his fridge
into limb-devouring sludgemolds.

His lover disappeared,
her whole apartment sucked
away in a freak storm
of subatomic singularities.

Her lover vanished when
a freak dip in quantum
flux teleported him
one kilometer too low.

Their quarrel ended forever
when they finally joined as one,
their matter/antimatter union
supernova hot, Big Bang bright.

A Million Layers Removed

Nothing is what it seems tonight;
unseen entities follow us, leaping
from rooftop to rooftop; the truck
rolls slowly past, windows black,
its engine whine the sinister hum

of flesh-seeking spacecraft.
Silhouettes of animals with two
legs too many scuttle between
the houses we pass; perhaps we've
passed through Riemann's cut,

ever-so-thin slit in the weave
of time and space, slipped into
a universe just a hair changed.
Or maybe I went through alone,
the woman with me now is

no longer you, and you walk on
in your own universe, with
a stranger. Perhaps we slip away
this way all the time, and you and I
are now a million layers removed,

never to meet again.

Requited

You killed me to keep me near.
Seven days, from then till now.
Why won't you kiss me, dear?

Your fingers squeezed my cries of fear
to silence as you kept your vow.
You killed me to keep me near.

You've slaked your needs yet now appear
so frozen — frightened — sweat-slicked brow.
Please, why won't you kiss me, dear?

Your heart in thorns, I've seen it clear,
this distance you could not allow,
until you killed to keep me near.

Your love's fire became my bier.
My arms reach for your warmth now.
Kiss my breath away, my dear.

My mouth on yours till I can't hear
your shrieks, ungrateful lover's row.
My tongue on yours, our fates cohere.
You killed me to keep me near.

lis pendens

I filed suit for your soul today
You felt the service in your bones
If by tonight you don't respond
Your spirit will become my own

Who will stop the judgment nigh
And represent you in your plight?
The counsel who will face this court
Cannot be hired in noonday light

So summoned, come, quaking *pro se*
And foolishly fight this complaint
The jury picked to hear your plea
Will not be stricken of my taint

No verdict cap or tort reform
Will curb the cost this judge demands
Once you've demurred and left your fate
Unbalanced in his scaly hands

I sued you for your soul this eve
And placed a lien upon your bones
No matter how just your appeal
Your spirit will become my own

The Strip Search

The Gate said "Abandon All Hope."

I thought I'd tossed all my hope away,
but when I stepped through the Gate, it still pinged.
One of the guards slithered out of its seat,
snarling as it drew forth a wand.
C'mere, it hissed,
it seems you're still holding out hope.

Its crusted hide was a Venus landscape up close.
It brushed that cold black wand all over my skin,
put it in places I don't want to talk about.
Snaggle fangs huffed in my face:
Sir, step over here, please.

Then the strip search began.
My flesh rolled up & tossed aside for mushy sifting.
Bones X-rayed, stacked in narrow rows, marrow
sucked out, tested, spit back in.
They made me open mind, heart, soul, shook them out
like sacks of flour, panned the contents
for every nugget of twinkling hope, glistening courage;
applying lethal aerosol
to any motion that could be ascribed to love or will
or malingering dreams —
sparing only a few squirming morsels
for later snacking.

Once they were done
they made me pick up my own pieces

(I did the best I could without a mirror)
then my guard kicked me out —
with a literal kick —
sent me rolling down the path to my final destination.

I'll be honest with you, it's no picnic here.
But, my friends, I still have hope. I do.

I'm not going to tell you
where I hid it.

Ectoppliances

No one here but me hears the burned-out Hoover
always whining unseen in the next room,
or my grown daughter's childhood dolls
that whisper taunts from her bedroom:
let's go shopping, let's be friends,
feed me, mama, I'm hungry.

How can I explain all these nights
spent sleepless, how the dryer
thumps and cackles and buzzes in the basement,
unaware I put it curbside years ago?
Or why I cover my ears on the bus ride
past the junkyard, so I can't hear
how the crushed ones scream and laugh?

Or how the cartoon clock I once owned
when I was five sometimes will try
to comfort me, its tick-tock whisper
rising from the babble,
like a mother's heartbeat
in the encroaching dark.

Mrs. Rigsby's Fatecast

A flurry of coronaries in the overnight forecast,
so watch what you're putting in those arteries
and try not to get too stressed out over nothing.

Those dark clouds of fate on the horizon
could mean accident precipitation, so be alert
if you're commuting home, and if you're someone
who works with industrial machinery, well,
don't put any body parts where they shouldn't be.

Our cancer alert remains in effect
for the 1,803rd straight day (since we've been
on the air, in fact): smokers take heed!

And if you happen to be Mrs. Hilda Rigsby,
do not walk down Coralview Avenue at 10:38
this evening. In fact, don't go anywhere near
that street, not even to satisfy your curiosity
as to why you've been warned away
from a place you've never heard of.

Consider this a special gift from our fatecasters to you.
Mrs. Rigsby, we hope you're watching us tonight.

No One

I do not hear a tapping
beside me at the window.
I will not raise the shade.
I will not see eyes there,
silver with reflected moonlight,
the same eyes that flashed

outside the attic window
as I peered up the dark stairwell
three long nights ago.
What face could have those eyes?
It doesn't matter, I tell myself.
I did not see them.

The scratching on the pane
I hear is just a branch
striking the glass.
There is no tree
next to my window,
but listen how the wind breathes —

it must have blown a branch down
from elsewhere in the yard.
The noise is relentless,
but tonight I'll leave it be,
stay here in my pool of light,
with my bookshelves and papers

and the comforting sounds
of my fingers on the keys.
There is no need
to indulge this growing impulse
to reach out, tug the shade,
unlatch the sash.

There is no pale face
waiting in the dark.
No one is screaming.

for Thomas Ligotti

Assembling Zembla

When the massmind's need for escape
    took form at last,
Nabokov's imaginary kingdom
    monikered it best —
but escapees encountered more,
    here in Zembla,
than *Pale Fire's* author ever
    could have wished for.
Fair towers crowned with
    lewd and lecherous gargoyles;
dragons in the secret tunnels,
    pupils palely aflame;
royal court dramas complicated
    by assassins composed
    of shadow and air;
and every daydreaming soul
    that fulfilled the role
    of Fairy Princess,
discovered keys to their chambers
    in the hands of serpent men
    with mundane knives.

Planeta do Favela

They meant well, perhaps they did,
preserving our tribes in sleep stasis
on vast *naves estrela* hovering in sky —
our entire land swallowed by their shadows.

They plucked seeds from life *Amazonia*
before last *florestas* burned and fell,
while ships bore our species to eco, to regrow,

cut us from dying stems and planted
us again on this climate-controlled *planeta*,
this cracked, dry world where they force

the sky to blue, graft the soil to brown,
pump green into stalks that have never quite
taken root. We live in what slums

they grow for us, we hunt in false forests,
play *palada* in the streets; and beg our keepers
to heal our mother-Earth, transplant us,

sink our roots home again — our queries met
with rainstorm patter of *políticos*
that echoes sewn-lipped silence of the dead.

The Captive Pleads with the

Please let me tell you, Knifeman,
what to take, what to leave,
if the blade you will wield through my brain
could be so delicate, leaving
sun and swingsets and books read
by the nightlight's illumination;
if you could, if you could;

Leave me the boys with the long sticks
who chased me along the street,
the sun beating down like my feet on the pavement;
Leave the blood that poured down my face
like a waterfall, loosed by a bully's well-aimed stone;
Leave all the awkward moments, the many,
where I, who understood numbers and cells
and particles and gravity but misunderstood
hints and cues, fumbled my words,
spoke too long, wore out attention spans and patience;
Leave the sneers, the annoyed stares of peers.

Please, Knifeman, don't mince me in
with the masses;
I don't want to believe that I
was ever ordinary.

Memory Carver

Your first taste of chocolate,
first exploring touch
of the white hot light bulb,
first wet kiss with your
second-grade sweetheart, these
we can auction, recoup
the value we've lost with you.

Some we will distill for study;
the snickers of peers and
snide derision (or sly approval)
of instructors that stirred
this unhealthy need to assert;
the swingset reveries
inventing unnecessary realms
of animal gods and hero swords
and perilous escape;
signs of the failure to
peacefully, productively interface.

The rest, we'll
scrape away, poured out
like so much garbage,
disposed of and done.

Midnight Rendezvous, Boston

The satyr lounges on the hotel lobby sofa,
one hoof dangled over the carpet of endless
fleurs-de-lis. Men and women in long black coats
stumble past, in flight from the flash-freeze winds
hidden in Boston's flurries; they crawl up the stairs,
weighed down by liquor and the doorman's gaze.

The satyr's eyes track a waitress's slit skirt
as she hurries outside for a forbidden smoke.
He smiles, paws the carpet, runs an idle ebony hand
through his curls of beard. No one
meets his gaze or looks his way.

The revolving door squeaks; his horned head turns
to look at the haughty antlers crowning the beast
bearing down on him, with its mantle of leaves
hung on shoulders strong as trees,
its hide of soft fawn down stretched taught
across an iron-muscled chest. The Horned One twirls
his javelin, impatient, stares down his snout
as the satyr reaches out, traces playful fingers
down the groove of the avatar's hard belly. No one
stops or asks them to stop — in Boston,
your kinks are not our business.

Later, the janitor pauses, appalled
at the animal noises from the restroom stall.
Someday they'll take out all the doors in here, he thinks,
and goes on about his business.

Midnight Rendezvous, Philly

Truth be told, we picked her up in Wilmington.
She told us she could guide us to the Vet,
wheedle a deal to keep us from the nosebleeds and
perch us near El Comedulce and Penthouse Pat.

She handed me my wallet in the lobby —
"You dropped this" — as I ogled two-tone hair,
nose and navel rings, square jacket, scarlet smile.
My buddy whispered "Hooker!" in my ear.

I asked why she limped; her wince: "In these boots,
wouldn't you?" Smirking like an imp. My friend
guffawed, but mere salacious fascination didn't
explain her appeal; enigmas beneath, an open-ended

question. So we stowed her on our quest, exotica,
unspoken tension — would we pay, if so
what would she do? She passed the crowded highway
miles with chatter, but I never seemed to know

what she just said, or the colors of her irises,
which I glimpsed, again, again, forgot, frowned at
my buddy, who nodded along as if nothing mattered.
"Phillies play the Cubs today. Sosa at the bat,"

he grinned as our Scheherezade announced that we
should take this exit coming up. Lo, and behold,
we descended into Philly, soon hopelessly lost
on streets crazy as scribbles. Her pout as we scolded:

"I used to know, like the back of my hand." She licked
there, like a cat. We asked a cop for directions but
somehow forgot as night fell. How many hours past
before we pulled up by the docks, scaffolds jutting

into the diamond sky above the Delaware,
black ships, mutant heads of leviathans,
watching as we drove. She told us how unseen
knives stabbed her feet, told how oceans

still call out to her, and she to them, as we
drove off the peer to meet her kith and kin,
our car filling fast with the flow of her chatter,
my buddy nodding along as if none of it mattered.

Midnight Rendezvous, Eden

—Won't you let me in, honeysweet, it's cold.
Her smile, shy, desperate, as she stood
in my motel room's doorway. —We'll have such a good
time. I'm wet for you. See?
                      She took hold
of her billowing T-shirt, lifted it to show
the tinny flesh beneath, the coiling
springs, machine parts glistening in oily
eager sheen . . . —You must want to know
what it feels like, you won't believe it.
                             I shook
my head to clear it, recited as a psalm
It's only a dream until she took my palm
and placed it *there*. Under my hand hooks
latched and gears spun. I didn't scream.
                          Her eyes
moistened with tears as I turned her away.
How can she cry, I wondered, surely that's a mask? —Okay,
she said. In a blink she vanished, the starless sky
dimming, shadows eclipsing the moon.

                        The next day,
I drove Eden's deserted streets past emptied factories,
eyeless smokestack hulks, shells of rural industry,
humbled dreams lying dead in every doorway,

abandoned in the search for cheaper alchemies.
Her face etched in crumbled brick and peeled paint,
framed through sagging glass in crooked window panes,
regarded me. Sad whispers warmed the breeze.

**staring down the sun:
the end he never sees**

Defacing the Moon

Your ship's sharpened keel
slides across airless seas,
blown by the breath of your desires.

Those sails stretch like skin
to catch the winds of your whimsy,
and the keelblade carves crags
into cheekbones and eyes.

Soon your own face will rise
from the moon's far side,
awaken and stare down the sun.

Freebasing the Moon

Seek the pusher in the bands
of shadow cordoning the trees.
Silver glitters in his cratered eyes,
pockets pregnant
with moondust in dimebags.
He dangles one,
flicks it so the residue settles,
holy manna from an astronaut's boot.

Once was, for the thrill he sells,
you signed away a soul.
Now it's cheap as a little blood
left dripping on the holly, a grope
swiftly ended beneath hawthorn spines,
or the bark peeled from a memory
that matters to no one but you:
see it come to life and wriggle
in his stunted hands.
His rat teeth flash, reflections
of the glow from your bag.
Draw your hood tight, and don't let his fingers
press against yours too long.

Soon barricaded in the closet
of your room, alone
with the famished dark; pull the spoon
from your mouth, let something sour
drip into your dreams and burn
a page to set the mixture boiling.
Savor this dollop of alchemy,

this dribble of ectoplasm, your voyage
beyond the coral shelf
of the bloodstream. The boosters
have survived the launch,
no need for a new needle.
But the expedition always ends too soon.

Sackful of Satellites

Brightness tossed from a silk sack spins in the wind, flashing light to dark to light and back again, caught in your palms and it shines cold, no heavier than a coin for Charon. The man with the sack skips away, long nightcap trailing behind, robes fluttering pale as ghost wings, black afterimage fades to grey. Treasure his gift against your heart as it starts to grow; but drop it before it swells too heavy, bores a hole in your earth, pulls in the tides like blankets.

Retracing the Moon

Hung in the sky, scratched to blank —
so many faces sculpted in dust,
one after another till all fell away,
till there remains only a template,
an empty stand, bald and bare.

I cup the moon in my hands,
lift it from its hook and balance
its weight in wheel and lathe.
I prepare to press fingers in
its silver skin, but think again.
Who am I to cook the clay of dreams?

I will forge you in no image,
round canvas for the wizards
to project all their craters,
seas and histories;
for the lovers to draw desire,
cast lures to pull their own tides;
for the atheist to worship,
prostrate before mindless rock,
while believers dissect and analyze:
filling their centrifuge
with reflected light,
spinning to distill God's face.

Anointing the Time Shark

The sanest of all madmen
built a church at Time's End.
Gothic spires challenged
the black hole sky.

Sanctuary rafters
so like whale's ribcage;
basilica buttresses
spread wide as fins.

Choir walled behind an altar,
conscripts from The Last Museum,
Men, women of all Epochs:
Earless futurians, almond-eyed;
Neanderthals with sloping brows;
Mu Magicians, Dreamtime shamans,
Mithraic priests, American witches
all raise their voices
in paranormal arias,
that shake a pair of clocks
flanking chancel's cross —
such hymns from variegated throats,
forced by this renegade conducter
who waves his wand as Final Storm
rages outside, tsunami aftershocks
from the Universe that refused
to choose its suicide (no Heat Death,
no Big Crunch, only Indecision
Cataclysm) and unleased
backward blasts of thwarted Time.

The madman intends to survive.
Exotic captive spirits
hit notes bent in new dimensions,
change the shape of this vessel
that held our mad saint's mind.

Now he knew light would never die.
Now he knew the Savior Cells
would trigger primal tides,
kill Death itself, reshape its bones,
ascend a new Host to its throne.
Leviathan fit for Floods of Ages.

As his body dissolves,
paired clocks become eyes.
Choir transcends into rows
Of teeth. Nave into gullet.
Stones into scales.
Our church flexes its tail
and launches vast and hungry
into Time's maelstrom.

Petting the Time Shark

An endless line of instants swims past,
interlocking scales, aimed in one direction,
a kaleidoscope of temptation; reach out,
slide your hand into the future.
Feel the flux of time against your palm,
unyielding fluid, flow of glass;
Stroke, always forward, never back,
never force your hand into the past,
lest it split, fragment, lay raw nerves
                open to history.

Eating the Time Shark

of course, in the end, it will eat you
with unkindest of kisses
your teeth, tongue, face, brain
sliding down its endless gullet

but though it's at best uneven comfort
there is space for skilled teeth to fight the current —
room, if you're fleet enough
to dine on your own fate

the pilot fish that swims alongside
the remora that attaches and rides
the lamprey that slices and bleeds
can you be stronger, swifter, more precise than these?
braving backwash and undertow
incising forward between the instant-thin
scales of history?

then masticating crosstime,
most delicate and diverse of all meals:
savoring the steak
more like a hallucinatory scotch
than any meaty texture
a burst of primaeval mud upon the mind's palate
followed by crackle of wood igniting
feral taste of iron, copper taste of blood
grit of concrete, bubbles of steam
stickiness of plastic topped with electric prickles
and aftertaste of diesel and silicon

bite deeper, deeper yet:
can you explore
the sweetness of a forming sun
bitter nebulas
the incomprehensible flavor
of the unexploded big bang

eternally starving parasite
can you burrow your way out of time?
can you burn your self to nothing
before you're swallowed?

The Hollow Sphere

Beneath my crown lounges
a pantheon of small and desperate gods,
their smooth flesh grown cracked and seamed
for want of each others' attentions;

My jackal-headed wit flashing her fangful grin
at no one and nothing; her silent yellow-eyed
sidekick nervously peeling his silky pelt raw;
the swollen one that fills an alcove
curls his elephant trunk, giggles softly
and tsks his shame. Spray of water
on his knee from the huge fish gasping
on the floor, jaw crippled from its own weight, the hour hand
in its eye twisting backward painfully.
A sad moon liked a discarded toadstool
strains to lift a face scarred by boots.

And these skeletal people crawling among them —
who are these grovelers in stained robes?
Any demon worth its salt would call them provender.

I will my starving avatars
to eat these pathetic cavern children
who stopped feeding us with love,
whose stale blood shall be poor substitute
no better than unleavened bread,
their flesh dry as paper spewed
from ash-clogged machines,
but enough to keep us alive till Oasis arrives.
Her voice tells me I speak in symbols

only my own small gods can read.
I tell this sorry Oracle my hosts are blind.

Only one power shines beneath this cemented dome,
burns Lucifer bright, pure hatred pulsing.
See how these godlings give their lives,
steam of spirit rising from beast-headed bodies,
whorling into One,
weaving the gravity of rage.

This shall grind
the bones of the followers with the pestle of its will.
This will split
the Oracle's face, spit sand in the screaming wound.
This will sculpt a new, drooling face
from the moon's erupting peaks,
this will goad the elephant god to fly,
this will give the shark's clockwork jaws
the strength to ratchet closed.

Escher's Bed

Procrustes cursed him from the underworld.
No sleep ever came without brutal struggle —
his mattress seemed to tilt the wrong way,
no matter which end he laid his head upon.

Poor sleepless boy, doomed to fail school,
sent by his vexed parents to live seaside
for his health (to no avail) but the dreams,
the longing for order, for symmetry,

spilled through his hands to crystallize
in press and ink. To Jetta (poor, tolerant wife)
he blamed those ever restless nights
on Rome, on his brother's body broken

on the mountainside, on the Nazi bootprint
found marring a sketch by his murdered
Jewish mentor — while the interlocking beasts
crawling across his prints mirrored the peace

Procrustes' hex denied him. Only when he
found the impossible object, the endless stair
that spirals up to meet its own beginning,
did he understand his torment, know

that on meeting the thief in Hades,
he must stretch and shorten in one stroke
to finally fit in his own bed, beside which
his family gathered to watch him descend,

holding Ariadne's thread as it spiraled
beyond the page, into the infinite.

Miró's Mirror

He discovered it, antique and strange,
in the cellar of that moss-veined farmhouse;
propped it in the corner of his secret studio,

where he stood, transfixed as Narcissus,
regarding the average, his father's forceful etching:
flat face, narrow shoulders, short timid legs,

every bit the accountant his father sculpted,
streaked by desperate stains of paint; he made
the vow, again, again, to unbind himself

from the ordinary; and through the other side,
things heard, converged from Catalan countryside,
things once seen only in dreams of peasants.

Behind him animals of line and riot
frolicked in midair; disembodied eyes opened
in blue beyond his window — never there

when he turned, but always in the glass,
too flat for any eyes but his to see, cavorting
in and out of frame like microbes under the lens.

He stared for hours, days; let them infect his retinas
till he saw, as they, how opacity of walls or skin
were mere parlor tricks, how his face, his house,

the farm outside, the world itself stood open
as the sky; how life's residual glow, bright corona,
clings to possessions simple as forks or shoes.

On the fourth night he went to sleep starving
and they invaded his dreams. Next morning,
the mirror gone, but from then on, they followed

in window reflections, in puddles, in corners
of a watering eye, shape shifting entourage,
endless carnival in orbit around his grasping soul.

He welcomed them, longed his life to join
their number, trade his skin for writhing, fluxing line,
unwinding hues which can no more be contained

than pagan dances of the frenzied spirit.

Tanguy's Pebble

They thought de Chirico granted him the gift, and he
allowed everyone to believe, because the truth was far
too strange. He never shared it, not even with Kay,
until too late:

parted from his ship off the Argentine coast,
stolen by the sea gods, delivered, thirsty and freezing,
into the shadow of the Patagonian forest, where a serpent
like coils of fire punctured him in greeting; overhead

the arboreal sea rolled, as he crawled in delirium
over rocky mounds like glowing coral, slipped with a gasp
into sudden grottos, into a world of air like water,
      of wonders:

beings of plasma and stone; ribbons of curling intellect
      distilled
from form or purpose; entities of gem-hued mercury flowing
against each other in couplings of love or death; up or down

cast away like masts in a storm, no horizon, unbounded chasm,
warm gold-green stretching beyond sight; he swum, spun,
center of new cosmos, observer of infinities, himself
      observed —

a small thing, a pebble of liquid, no larger than a lima bean
drifted near, hovered at his fingertips like an inquisitive cat.
Anemone in miniature, his fingers closed — he felt little more
than a soap-bubble burst; fingers splayed again, the pebble
      gone.

All warmth extinguished. The universe, a roiling blue abyss.
Great hairy worm-things squealed, bleeding clouds of
         octopus ink.
Needle pyramids stabbed the void; wires like marionette
         strings
grew from nowhere, angled toward him, groped for his limbs.

He fled, in no direction and all, steered by fear beyond
         understanding,
to rouse, thrashing, in sheets soaked with ocean brine
         sweat; daylight
leaned in over the strange adobe arches of Rio Gallegos.
         Naked,
he stood before the mirror, a sea-hardened merchant
         mariner, Bible

perched by the basin like an accusation; stood, watched
         movement
beneath his skin, a throbbing lump the size of a pebble,
         submerged
into the meat below his wrist. No pain in his flesh, but an ache
that grew, a wanderlust no longer sated by waves against
         a hull

or foreign ports filled with women of exotic skins. His return
to Paris failed to ease that formless urge, till he read Breton,
felt hope stir. At first his efforts were crude, amateur-Dali,
but his pebbled hand, no matter how he fought, grew more
         sure,

opening windows to boundless regions he began to see
as home: underwater dreamscapes, crawling crystal cities,
peopled with animalcules of molten stone. He married
         troubled Kay,
herself adrift, who sensed how his soul trawled the deeps,

but couldn't share his mercurial bond, her paintings
      imperfect
refractions of that subtidal realm. Yet powers there sensed
their congregation of two, warned them of what leered from
over the Alsace; he saw it in the midst of a picnic, black cloud

hovering in the east, grinning, amoebic, exploded cubist
      skull —
or perhaps a different warning caused his westward flight.
Ensconced in America, he forced his dreams a different way,
exchanging water and crystal for desert and meshing line,

a new space where, perhaps, he hoped to slip away when
the marionette wires latched to him at last; resigned,
      homesick,
he put up no fight as they dragged him away, leaving poor Kay
to pore in confusion over the quicksilver pebble left behind,

that lodged in her arid dreams like the bullet
in her broken heart.

Klee's Garden

The objective world surrounding us
is not the only one possible;
there are others, latent.

Only the most beloved
of his Bauhaus pupils ever
were allowed to frolic there;
and perhaps the models who caught his eye:
Emma, Thérèse, Kathi, Mari, more —
Surely Lily knew; he denounced
painting from life years before,
though maybe his requests
were nothing so simple as amorous affairs.
(And how often did he take *her* there?
Afterward, could she speak of it?
Could she even remember?)

What strange blooms assaulted his senses
at the edge of the Sahara;
an unwise venture southward of Carthaginian ruins,
wrapped by heat that strove to turn
his flesh to paper; the miracle wind
that parted sands like so much troublesome sea;
stone temple bones protecting impossible flora,
square petals of light that, rubbed against his
vision, transmuted before his very eyes —
He dashed back from Tunisia
weeks too early, mind on fire —
The friend he left behind might also
have seen the miracle, but a French mortar shell
bought August Macke's silence.

Color has taken possession of me;
No longer must I chase after it.
I know it has hold of me forever.

The seeds, pure motes of holy hue,
sewn in the dour woods south of Weimar,
secluded even from the seclusion of his school.
At the garden grew, he meditated alone —
The Buddha of Bauhaus — coming back
with cryptic theories of design, encrypted in a grimoire
only true initiates had a hope of grasping;

perhaps that need to communicate drove him to share.
Tiny man with Rasputin's stare, mere hint
of the unearthly glow he absorbed in Africa;
as he led them on scant path through brush,
were his eager protégés ever unnerved —
their unease growing as colors amplified;

around the next turn, ancient trees reduced
to sprightly line and flimsy planes of pigment,
rippling, overlapping, mixed into new shades
by slightest puffs of air; even odder luminous growths
defining themselves against inexplicable shadows;
then the landscaping he himself applied:
cacti incongruous as tubular totems, flower pots
out of airborne boats, rows
of sawblade sun blooms; and then,
clearer moment by moment, movement:
the residents, creatures sideways from human —
Residue, perhaps, of the lucky few
he chose to let in: women with faces like blowing leaves,
men with numbers for eyes, clothed
like stop-motion phantoms;

(Beneath it all, deep underneath,
did his guests perceive the not-quite angel

with the pig-snout and pit-black orbits,
or the round-faced German whose eyes
and nose and mouth spelled "death";
or the desert itself, watching for
its chance to reclaim, to dry his flesh
from inside out, mummified in diseased agony?
He noted them from time to time
and merely instructed his wide-eyed companions
to ignore the degenerates.)

Who could then resist, when he
produced his violin and sent the notes flying
like a calculated sandstorm?
Majestic gold or courtesan blue,
flowers leapt fishlike into the air —
blocks of rainbow adobe
became spontaneous houses, temples, mosques;
bipeds covered in square scales
stood up to sing, as whimsical creatures
danced in their translucent bellies,
swallowed whole and joyous.
Among them all, he pranced,
most benevolent of all devils,
legs blurred as he scrambled up ladders,
slid down stalks, his fiddle bow
drawing mad black lines on the very
cloth of time, and he called out names
that hung rapturously beside him,
sound become tangible calligraphy.

Who could help but laugh
and clap hands in delight?
Who could help but lose themselves,
leave a piece behind?

I cannot be understood
in purely earthly terms.

Chagall's Lamp

She shone from inside,
her skin like sunlit clouds,
her eyelashes pins of light.
He followed her, his beacon,
to escape the grey lands,
to emerge in the world each morning.

Simple man who wore
the ghosts of his beloved Vitebsk
like a comforting shawl;
because he knew they weren't ghosts at all.
Reduced to ruins by Nazi hands,
but he found it again
the first time he followed her
beyond the grey lands.

She first revealed herself to him
long years before
he left the black and white of Russia
for the kaleidoscope of Paris:
in days when his world held nothing more
than carts and cows and long school hours,
and dreams of magic-colored laughter.

At first he thought her nothing more
than his beautiful Bella
perceived in spirit by his yearning soul:
lounging nude atop
the roses on the mantle;
staring up at him from puddles,

a distaff reflection;
beheld in nighttime visions,
borne away on horses
by shadowy barbarians,
or towering anxiously over
infinities of forest where fey children played.

But he knew her to be something more
when every sighting became the same:
a shining figure cut from a summer sky,
kneeling alone, head bowed,
solemn as his mother praying at the synagogue,
a steady lamp in a vast plain of shifting grey.

She stayed with him in Moscow and Berlin,
and the creative tempest of the Paris streets.
He watched her each night, but
kept his distance, more awed than afraid.
She stayed with him, when the Stalin plague,
then the Blitzkrieg,
walled his childhood home away.

When he and Bella fled to America,
when the message came, surreal psychic telegram,
that Nazis hollowed out his beloved town;
that's when he overcame his awe,
when he spoke to her, when she stood,
beckoned him to follow
through the grey lands, past
the smiling red-eyed soldiers, past
the white crucifix leaning above the ruins.

Past all that, and there they were,
breathing in strange new space:
green-faced violin players guarding
vertical streets; carts full of children flying

above rooftops, pulled by manic nags
whose foals romped among stars;
men and women unclothed, unbound
by flesh or gravity, finding untried ways
to interlock; quiet Jews robed in earth
and light, still insisting on prayer;
winged jugglers with hummingbird heads
and wide sympathetic eyes;
all things freed of black and white
to be seen as they always truly were.
His own eyes brimming, he raised
his hands — now seven-fingered —
blew kisses to her glowing form in gratitude.

He built monuments to her in glass,
the light he knew as hers filtered
through the tints of the true universe
which he saw at first hand each night
beyond the grey lands.

The final time he followed her,
as age, infirmity, uncertainty
slipped from him like a snake's skin,
he flowed across the space between them,
touched her at last, pressed flowers
into her warm, beaming hands.

Blood-red fauns and sea-blue nymphs
danced around his naked body and hers
at their wedding feast.

Picasso's Rapture

Aphrodite is exacting a tribute of me for all my race.
— Ovid, *Heroides*

1. *une femme*

There is no abstract art.
You must always start
with something. Afterwards
you can remove all traces of reality.

By the time of their meeting, he
was indeed a Master.
Removing her reality
took no more effort
than sketching a face on air.

The Minotaur's passion sated,
he left her a twisted, flattened shell,
curled like wet canvas on his padded chair,
mouth soundlessly screaming
from the same side of her face
that both eyes now started from.

He sighed in satisfaction,
then began the erasure.
Soon, no one there.
As with many before her.
He had not learned her name,
and did not care.

2. *son visage bleu*

Casagemas' head protruded
from the sheet that wrapped his
body; eyelids swollen,
temple stained black with
gunpowder, skin blue and
waxen in the candlelight.

Pablo watched them bear away
his best friend from Barcelona,
slain by a woman's refusal
as surely as she'd tugged his
fingers on the pistol with
puppet strings. Pablo knew
then: all women are witches.
Only an equal sorcerer
can survive them.

When the scarlet fever delirium
claimed him from Madrid,
he had lain in a down-stuffed bed
in a Catalonian mountain villa,
staring through a narrow window
at the verdant slopes; things seen
in that haze, shapes cavorting
in mid-air, opening doors
that weren't there, opening
space to show him views
from all angles at once.
Memories gnawed at the back
of his grieving brain: how to
find again that visionary state,
force it to obey his desires?

Until he found the first hints,
Casagemas' blue face swelled
behind every new encounter.

3. *l'Arlequin*

Some claim he infused those
thousands of canvasses with
hidden arcana, invocations
au culte mithraïque, tributes
to the god who slew
the celestial bull; had he heard,
Pablo would have laughed,
and rightly so, for the only alchemy
fused into his creations
was a magic he alone invented.

Against the skin of Fernande,
his first mistress, and first woman
he would claim to truly love,
the rapture of seeing outside
space returned, this time
to a clear, unfevered mind,
and he knew he could be
the new Harlequin, protégé
of trickster Hermes, author
of any wizardry his lusts demanded.

He painted himself,
handsome, sullen, clad in
diamonds of rose and black,
wearing Harlequin's peaked hat,
the nature of his magic
as yet unsculpted. He filled
the following years with a quest

for final configurations,
sharpened the vision that saw
from all sides at once, allowed
him to shape others to his whim.

And at last he shed
the Harlequin's chequered skin;
pierced and thrown away
with the toss of a horn
as he assumed the form
(distilled from the arenas
of Spain) that suited him best.

4. *Minotauromachia*

Do all women harbor a need
for annihilation? Most would deny it
but if one did yearn, he would find her,
smell her an auction hall away,
taste her scent amid hundreds
in the newly-opened gallery,
home in on her through
crowded streets; the Minotaur
weaving toward its meal.

As helpless as Europa draped
across the bull, she would come
to where he led, brook no struggle
as the Beast compressed,
flattened, conformed her
to its all-consuming vision.

Why not the genitals
in place of the eyes,
and the eyes between the legs?

Even those whom he allowed
names, whom he spared
the Bull's machinations:
what of them? One hanged,
two driven insane, one shooting
herself (just as Casagemas);
others that survived live on
only in the story he painted.

5. *son seul amour vrai*

How to reconcile the cocky hero
whose heart tore at the thought
of a Basque village bombed,
who painted a protest of
war's horrors, pressed postcards
of that protest into the hands
of Nazi soldiers, and yet
was never arrested; could the same
man be the Beast who tore
scores of women into surreal
contortions, and casually disposed
of the remains? Could one
divide himself so completely
into parallel planes?

Though he once imagined it so,
no avenging angel with hawk beak
and barrel chest ever descended
to stuff the Minotaur back
in its Harlequin cloak, bear
the wailing creature away.

Though he uttered the word
too many times to count,

only one woman truly earned
his adoration. As he lounged
in the Chateau Vauvenargue,
he recognized her form,
sensuous curves out of his
deepest dreams drawing into
focus. He readied himself
for the one mistress
that remained to conquer
or at last be bested by,
knowing he loved her truly,
knowing she loved him even more.

I think of Death all the time.
She is the only woman
who never leaves me.

Pollock's Knives

He fell into the painting — Jack the Dripper
poured his self out, used broken glass
to thicken the medium, attacked the surface
from all four sides. The careening convertible

at last came to a stop, but he did not, not yet —
his blood so much flying pigment,
quicksilver droplets, suspended —
He gave up completely and so achieved
complete control.
                   He fell into the painting
that opened around him in all directions.
He fell into the universe of his dying,
god and sacrifice all in one.
                   Was his goddess
anywhere to be found, the moon woman
with crescent pupils, who tore apart the circle
of her own binding while he watched?

His mistress would survive the car crash.
His wife would survive the wreck of his life.
His last thoughts in this world weren't
for them at all.

* * *

He had at last found what to do
when he couldn't paint:
a proper death for an American celebrity,
cementing immortality by casting life aside.

He controlled the ebb and flow,
but things always changed
once they struck the surface.

* * *

Broiling boy, never knew
a home, a proper place; if

a surface seemed stable, he would
assault it, abrade it,
shatter it, shred the pieces.
Struggling mother Stella tried
to harness his fury, focus it
on canvas. But a canvas
couldn't cry out in pain.
His life a chaos of turbulence,
something vulnerable always
bleeding at its off-center.

Fight in an L.A. alley,
this one involved knives.
The small Mexican boy
had black eyes, coal black,
(no whites) and two arms
too many to defend against;
vanished, left his blades broken
off in 16-year-old Paul's
screaming flanks (that name, Paul,
he later shed, reverse-Saul) but no one else
could see the wounds he claimed were there;
or they would not admit it,
no matter how he insisted.

An art school in New York:
as far away from those black orbs as he could go.

The alcohol forever walled away
the memory of that strange encounter
but not its effects.

He tried to bleed himself.
Relieve the piercing pressure
that wormed in deeper every day.
At first he didn't know the way.

He searched Mexican murals,
with their dark-eyed martyrs,
though he didn't understand what answer
he was looking for.

When Miró's phantasms and Picasso's distortions
erupted in the museum halls,
he felt resonance, kinship, a sense
of distance closed, of surfaces gone brittle,
primed to be shattered.

The alcohol walled the ways,
but rage superceded stupor, forced him
to climb, search blind
for the way to bleed himself.

* * *

She didn't look human, couldn't have been,
creature whose face
was the moon turned away from the sun.
(Afterward, he would paint her,
though he couldn't articulate her form,
understood it wasn't wise to try.)
Sigils of constellations

coalesced at her back
into a word he could not fathom.
How deep had he crawled inside himself,
to find her here?

She was bound inside a circle of her own making,
or of his: a sense of struggle, frozen, poised,
but then something —
the essence of a knife, blurred blade
in the abstraction of her hand.
The circle lashed away, snapped free,
crumpling to a flowing loop of blood-black.

She stared at him and at the same time stared away
through an eye with a bright crescent pupil
and an eye limned like ink scratched on sun
before dissolving into splotches, trickling off
and gone.
    He did not love her.
But knew in his cells what her message meant.

I will bleed all colors.
      I will control
the ebb and flow. I will paint with knives.

* * *

He tried to fall through the floor of his barn,
dripping, seeping across canvas after canvas,
attacking from all sides, slicing the excess
until only the perfect window remained,
or nothing at all. The ache left
for three beautiful years; happy years without walls.

But the blades did not come free,
would not; though he poured out more than

he could ever contain, some taint remained.
The ache returned, then the walls.
In the end he could not paint at all.

* * *

And at last he found what to do
when he couldn't paint.
No color was sufficient surrogate
for the hue he knew he had to use
to cremate the memory of black eyes.

As he tore apart the circle of his own binding,
did crescents open in his new sky?

His last thoughts in transition
plunged through an endless —
flooded with layer on layer
of streaking stars, seeping galaxies.
Things vast and multi-limbed
loomed beyond the edge, quasar echoes.

His last thoughts in transition
weren't human thoughts at all.
Things always changed
once they broke the surface.

O'Keeffe's Bones

To me they are strangely more living
than the animals walking around . . .
They cut sharply to the center of something
keenly alive — vast, empty, untouchable —
that knows no kindness with its beauty.

No god could survive in the desert.
But dead gods
still can desire. Speak. Scheme.

They watched this small woman
with black hair pulled back taut,
her easels and determined paints,
her square face and gaze
deep as endless horizons.

They watched this small fierce woman
who did not know them, yet still she was drawn
away from the claustrophobic loveliness of Lake George,
from the claustrophobic darkness of New York,
from Alfred's claustrophobic love.

They spoke to her in subtleties.
In black rocks, beveled cliffs, bleached ivory.
They schemed in sand red as raw flesh.
Undaunted by the stark Catholic crosses
that captured her eye,
they chose their moment, and
she saw:

a head of blunt teeth, empty sockets, withered hide;
its jagged-bone grin dwarfed the Black Hills' wrinkled face,
its multitude of antlers curled
into the space above sky,
great branches of bone
which could hold moons as trees dangle fruit.
Sky gathered thunderheads in a mantle,
soaked the emptiness
beneath its rolling cloak,
spoke of beauty in fragments,
of love scoured clean of the mortal,
of the perfection of the faraway,
sad and majestic as skeletal landscapes
from which she never fully returned.

From her Ghost Ranch
she worshiped
and in the end worshiped alone,
her faith enough to flood a desert
with umber, to fill cracks in stone
with black rivers,

to saturate sands
with the cooling blues of night;
to give driest rock the vitality
of arterial blood.

Mondrian's War

You cannot find his pain inside immaculate lines.
You cannot find the sleepless hours spent alone.
His brush moving non-stop till his fingers blistered;
a pause to double over in dry heaves; when done,
begin again, breath hitching; snot and tears
as unyielding stripes forced order on the primal;
sketched first on the page, each new cage designed
to perfect the prime balance.
                         But never perfected enough.
By the end, too much hung inside the scales for
his thoughts to ever rest or his hands to ever pause
as the sickness slowly thickened in his lungs.

When did he first discover this gift for equilibrium?
An urgent revelation in a haystack-mounded field?
Wind-swept grass arrayed behind his eyes in
primary bands of power? Lines like those that in
the next decade boys who lied about their age
would dig in mortar-scarred earth, premature men
doomed to spill their lives in mud.
                         As war raged,
he fought to smooth and contain; believing still
that harmony could be truth and truth harmony:
general beauty with utmost awareness. Abstraction
his new alchemy, a quest to reveal the bones
of the sublime, skeleton of black borders and
color fields; but the formulae eluded him;
ebony dulled to gray, lines retreated from the fronts,
forms refused the restrictions he imposed.

The war ended on its own, the shape he sought
still unknown.
            But the urgency, the need, never
abated, never relaxed its guard. He polished and
polished in Paris until the columns and ranks
held their place and refused to back away from
the boundaries. Endless variations inside diamonds
and squares: were they all pieces of larger patterns,
fragments of a design only his head could hold
in whole, these thaumaturgies schemed in paint?

Step up close and learn the fury of plain and plane.
Images that fool the eye into mistaking white space
for emptiness; but the brush strokes, running
in so many deliberate directions, explosive
kinetics craftily restrained within the bars,
energies controlled and composed, regimented
shards of the Great Order he strove to make
real in every line, but not in time; not in time.
Germany spilled out beyond its designated
shape and forged new emptiness from order,
drew vectors that would tear through fragile forms and
make colors bleed.
            Fugitive in New York:
each new painting a terrible labor, but his
efforts in between just as panicked; the panels
he hung on the studio walls, a set of eight
that he moved and moved and moved, and
constantly rearranged the colored squares
tacked within, searching for that balance,
that optimum interlace of energy. As the world
tilted further and further, he fought to tip it back.
One slender man in a draft-plagued room, battling
to flatten the violence, the vileness, even
as the effort turned to poison. Slowly dying, still
he arranged his squares until something resonated

in the very air, something he could feel
with his palms and call beauty, call pure.
Then, he would paint and paint until he wept.

The last, unfinished work: black lines replaced
with marching color, every simple square a shout
of joy. Had something shown him, even then,
the war's end he would never live to see?

Acknowledgments

"The Journey to Kailash" first appeared in *Strange Horizons*, Jan. 23, 2006.

"Tithonus on the Shore of Ocean" first appeared in *Change*, ed. John Benson, Not One of Us, 2006.

"Charon Finds a Woman on the Gridshore," first print appearance here.

"Sisyphus Walks" first appeared in *Goblin Fruit*, Issue 1, April 2006.

"Secret Infernos" first appeared in *Talebones*, Winter 2005.

"Bacchanal" first appeared in *Goblin Fruit*, Issue 3, Autumn 2006.

"Giving Back to the Muse" first appeared in *Goblin Fruit*, Issue 7, Autumn 2007.

"deathmask" first appeared in *Helix: A Speculative Fiction Quarterly*, Issue 7, Winter 2008.

"Time Triptych" first print appearance here.

"Petals" first appeared in *Star*Line*, Vol. 31, Issue 2, 2008.

"Saturn Devours His Children" first appeared in *Star*Line*, Vol. 24, Issue 2, 2001.

"The Golden Helmet" first appeared in *Disturbing Muses*, Prime Books 2005.

"Der Maulkorb," first print appearance here.

"The Thirteenth Hell," first print appearance here.

"Ghosts of the Apocalypse," first print appearance here.

"The Disturbing Muses" first appeared in *Disturbing Muses*, Prime Books, 2005.

"Manifest Density" first appeared in *Helix: A Speculative Fiction Quarterly*, Issue 2, Oct. 2006.

"The Asteroid Painter" first appeared in *Dreams & Nightmares* #67, 2004.

"A Curtain of Stars" first appeared in *Star*Line*, Vol. 25, Issue 5, 2002.

"Pulse" first appeared in *Strange Horizons*, Sept. 22, 2003.

"Black Holes Hold Their Breath" first appeared in *Abyss & Apex* #16, 2005.

"Watching the Pot" first appeared in *Scavenger's Newsletter*, Issue 157, March 1997.

"Strange Cargo" first appeared in *Strange Horizons*, Dec. 6, 2004.

"retrovirus" first appeared in *Illumen*, Vol.1, Issue 2, Spring 2005.

"Disaster at the Brainbank™ ATM" first appeared in *Talebones*, Oct. 1998.

"Munchausen vs. the Aliens" first appeared in *Talebones*, Spring 1998.

"The End of the Affair" first appeared in *Talebones*, Fall 2002.

"A Million Layers Removed" first appeared in *Tales of the Unanticipated* #23, 2002.

"Requited," first print appearance here.

"lis pendens" first appeared in *Strange Horizons*, June 26, 2006.

"The Strip Search" first appeared in *Strange Horizons*, Oct. 3, 2005.

"Ectoppliances" first appeared in *Tales of the Unanticipated* #21, 2000.

"Mrs. Rigsby's Fatecast" first appeared in *Strange Horizons*, Sept. 1, 2003.

"No One" first appeared in *Dreams & Nightmares* #62, 2002.

"Assembling Zembla" first appeared in *Altair* #5, 2000.

"Planeta do Favela" first appeared in *Defacing the Moon and Other Poems*, DNA Publications, 2000.

"The Captive Pleads With the Memory Carver" first appeared in *Tales of the Unanticipated* #26, 2005.

"Midnight Rendevous, Boston" first appeared in *EOTU Ezine*, June 2003.

"Midnight Rendevous, Philly," first print appearance here.

"Midnight Rendevous, Eden," first print appearance here.

"Defacing the Moon" first appeared in *Scavenger's Newsletter*, Issue 160, June 1997.

"Freebasing the Moon" first appeared in *Strange Horizons*, June 25, 2007.

"Sackful of Satellites" first appeared in *Lone Star Stories* 22, Aug. 2007.

"Retracing the Moon," first print appearance here.

"Anointing the Time Shark," first print appearance here.

"Petting the Time Shark" first appeared in *Tales of the Unanticipated* #23,

2002.

"Eating the Time Shark" first appeared in *Strange Wisdoms of the Dead*, Wildside Press, 2006.

"The Hollow Sphere" first appeared in *Lone Star Stories* 19, Feb. 2007.

"Escher's Bed" first appeared in *Star*Line*, Vol. 27, Issue 2, 2004.

"Miró's Mirror" first appeared in *The Pedestal Magazine* #24, 2004.

"Tanguy's Pebble" first appeared in *Disturbing Muses*, Prime Books 2005.

"Klee's Garden" first appeared in *Disturbing Muses*, Prime Books, 2005.

"Chagall's Lamp" first appeared in *Strange Horizons*, March 7, 2005.

"Picasso's Rapture" first appeared in *Strange Horizons*, June 6, 2005.

"Pollock's Knives" first appeared in *Disturbing Muses*, Prime Books, 2005.

"O'Keeffe's Bones" first appeared in *Disturbing Muses*, Prime Books, 2005.

"Mondrian's War," first print appearance here.

The author would like to thank the following individuals, without whose advice, encouragement and influence, this book and/or its contents would not exist: Laird Barron, John Benson, Nelson Bond, Harold Bose, Bruce Boston, Tyree Campbell, Tamathy Christensen, Ellen Datlow, Larry Dennis, Richard Dillard, Roger Dutcher, Amal El-Mohtar, Gary Every, Janet Fox, Vickie Holt, Mary Horton, Mardel James, Debbie Kolodji, David Kopaska-Merkel, Eric Marin, Laurie Mason, Robin Mayhall, Drew Morse, Tim Mullins, Vera Nazarian, John Peery, Tim Pratt, Kathryn Rantala, Cathy Reniere, Jody Rose, Charles Saplak, Marge Simon, Vandana Singh, Debbie Slagle, Christina Smith, Patrick Swenson, Sonya Taaffe, JoSelle Vanderhooft, Trent Walters, Ian Watson, Bud Webster, Jessica Wick, Laurel Winter, Dwayne Yancey; and of course, Anita.